Franklin's Christmas Gift

For Hannah and Charlotte Cowan,
two very special girls — P.B.

To my parents, for the warm Christmas memories — B.C.

Franklin is a trade mark of Kids Can Press Ltd.

ISBN 0-590-02611-9

All rights reserved. Published by Scholastic Inc., 555 Broadway, New York, NY 10012, by arrangement with Kids Can Press Ltd. SCHOLASTIC and associated logos are trade marks and/or registered trade marks of Scholastic Inc.

12 11 10 9 8 7 6 5   9/9 0 1 2 3/0

Printed in the U.S.A.   23

First Scholastic printing, November 1998

Franklin's Christmas Gift

Written by Paulette Bourgeois
Illustrated by Brenda Clark

SCHOLASTIC INC.

New York   Toronto   London   Auckland   Sydney
Mexico City   New Delhi   Hong Kong

FRANKLIN loved Christmas. He could name all of Santa's reindeer. He could tie ribbons into bows and play "Silent Night" on his recorder.

Franklin liked to give presents and to receive them. But this year he couldn't decide what to give to the Christmas toy drive.

Every December the students in Mr. Owl's class donated toys for needy families. The toys could be new or carefully used.

When Mr. Owl put out the collection box, everyone was excited. They had three days to choose the perfect gifts to give.

That evening Franklin dug through his toys.
He picked up a shiny red car.

"I remember this," he said, wheeling it around.
"Vroom!"

Next, Franklin pulled out a stuffed elephant
and held her tight.

"I wondered where you'd gone!" he cried.

Then Franklin found his best green marble. It had been missing for weeks.

"Fantastic!" he shouted.

Franklin loved his marbles. He had won every marble in his collection, and each one was beautiful.

Franklin picked through the rest of the toys. He decided to keep everything but a rusty truck with a missing wheel.

Franklin asked his father to help him fix the truck.

"We can try," said his father. "But it won't look new or even gently used."

"It's all I have. Everything else is too special to give away."

"I'd like you to think about that," said Franklin's father. "Christmas is a time to be generous."

The next day at school, Franklin asked his friends what they were giving.

Beaver was donating her big book of questions and answers.

"I already know all the answers," she boasted.

"I'm giving a puzzle," said Bear. "I only did it once."

Franklin frowned. "I'm giving a truck ... I think."

He had two days left to decide.

But Franklin was too busy to think about the toy drive.

He played the recorder in the school concert, made a card for Mr. Owl, and wrote a holiday story.

"I'll pick a toy after school," he promised himself.

When Franklin got home, there was a gift for him under the tree. It was from Great Aunt Harriet.

Franklin was so excited that he forgot all about choosing a gift for the toy drive.

Franklin squeezed the present and shook it.

"No peeking," laughed his mother.

"Do you know what it is?" asked Franklin eagerly.

"It must be something special." His mother smiled. "Great Aunt Harriet always gives presents that mean something to you and to her."

"Like last year," said Franklin.

Great Aunt Harriet knew that he loved to put on plays. And she gave him two puppets that had been hers when she was little. It was one of Franklin's best presents ever.

The next day at school, the collection box was brimming.

"You've all been very generous," said Mr. Owl. "Do you know that your gift might be the only one somebody receives this holiday?"

Franklin gulped. He'd never thought of that. He had to bring a present tomorrow!

Franklin raced home after school and looked through his toys again.

Somebody else might love Elephant, but she was worn from so much hugging.

And Franklin wasn't sure that the red car went fast enough.

Franklin was upset. At first, all of his toys had seemed too special to give away. Now, nothing seemed special enough.

Franklin played with his puppets and thought about how Great Aunt Harriet chose her gifts.

"The best presents are special to give and to receive," he whispered.

Then Franklin saw his marble collection and he knew that the marbles were special enough for the toy drive.

Franklin polished them and put them into a soft purple bag.

He wrapped the present and made a gift tag that read:

These are lucky marbles.
Merry Christmas.

The next morning, Franklin put his present on top of the collection box.

Then Franklin and his friends hauled the box to the big tree at the Town Hall.

They placed each present under the tree.

Franklin knew he would miss his marble collection. Still, he didn't feel at all sad. Instead, he felt good all over.

On Christmas Eve, Great Aunt Harriet came to visit and Franklin was allowed to open her present.

He ripped off the paper.

"It's perfect!" said Franklin. "Thank you."

Great Aunt Harriet beamed. She had made a stage for Franklin's puppet shows.

"Now open yours," Franklin insisted.

Great Aunt Harriet unwrapped her gift slowly and carefully.

Inside was a play, written by Franklin and dedicated to her.

"This is my best Christmas present ever," said Great Aunt Harriet.

Franklin got that good-all-over feeling one more time.